Visit us on the Web! www.randomhouse.com/kids

Educators and librarians, for a variety of teaching tools,
visit us at www.randomhouse.com/teachers

Library of Congress Cataloging-in-Publication Data
Mitton, Tony.
A very curious bear / by Tony Mitton ;
illustrated by Paul Howard. — 1st American ed.
p. cm.
Summary: A very curious bear asks his parent questions
about everything they see and do all day long.
ISBN 978-0-375-85083-7 (trade)
[1. Bears—Fiction. 2. Animals—Infancy—Fiction. 3. Curiosity—Fiction.]
I. Howard, Paul, ill. II. Title.
PZ8.3.M685Ve 2009
[E]—dc22
2008010142

MANUFACTURED IN CHINA
10 9 8 7 6 5 4 3 2 1
First American Edition

A Very Curious Bear

by **Tony Mitton** • illustrated by **Paul Howard**

Random House New York

These are the words that a little bear said
to a big bear one day as they got up from bed:

Why does the sun come
and light up the day?

To wake you from sleep
so you come out and play.

Why does the wind rush around in the air?

To fill you with joy and to blow away care.
(And maybe to tease you by ruffling your hair!)

Why does the path make such wriggles and bends?

To take us on journeys and lead us to friends.

Why does the stream seem to gurgle and babble?

It's whispering, "Dip in your toes for a dabble."

Why do the daisies squeeze up from the grass?

To drink in the light
as the dreamy days pass.

Why does the rain come
and wet the world through?

To help grow the things that we need to feed you.

Why does the sky go all rumbly with thunder?

To give us a shiver and fill us with wonder.

But why must the world fill with roaring and crashing?

It's the song of the storm, and the lightning flashing.

Why would the wind and the weather above
destroy such a beautiful thing that we love?

Bad things can happen that also bring good.
  Just look, there's a bridge where the old tree once stood.

But the sun's going down and the world's turning gray.
Let's try to be home by the end of the day.

Why is the moon like a lamp in the sky?

For light and for beauty, and wondering why.

But what am I meant for and why am I here?

To live and to wonder, my darling, my dear.

Where will I go when I sleep and I dream?

To the way through the woods by the whispering stream.

Then the curious bear gave a tired little yawn
and snuggled in bed and slept deeply till dawn.